Lily Allen

It's Not Me, It's You

PUBLISHED BY
WISE PUBLICATIONS
14-15 BERNERS STREET,
LONDON W1T 3LJ, UK.

EXCLUSIVE DISTRIBUTORS:
MUSIC SALES LIMITED
DISTRIBUTION CENTRE, NEWMARKET ROAD,
BURY ST EDMUNDS, SUFFOLK IP33 3YB, UK.

MUSIC SALES PTY LIMITED
20 RESOLUTION DRIVE, CARINGBAH,
NSW 2229, AUSTRALIA.

ORDER NO. AM997051
ISBN 978-1-84938-019-5

MUSIC ARRANGED BY JACK LONG.
MUSIC PROCESSED BY PAUL EWERS MUSIC DESIGN.
EDITED BY JENNI WHEELER.

ORIGINAL CD PACKAGING:
PHOTOGRAPHY BY SERGE LEBLON.
ART DIRECTION & DESIGN BY ALEX COWPER.
ART DIRECTION & COMMISSIONING BY DAN SANDERS.
SET DESIGN BY ANDY HILLMAN.

PRINTED IN THE EU.

WISE PUBLICATIONS
PART OF THE MUSIC SALES GROUP
LONDON / NEW YORK / PARIS / SYDNEY /
COPENHAGEN / BERLIN / MADRID / TOKYO

Everyone's At It

Words & Music by Lily Allen & Greg Kurstin

Dm F Am Dm F
1. I don't know much, but I know this for cer - tain, that is the sun
2. I get in - volved, but I'm not ad - vo - cat - ing. Got an o - pin-
Am Dm F
pok - in' his head 'round the cur - tain. Please can we leave,
- ion, yeah, you're well up for slat - ing. See, you've got a pres - crip -
Am Dm F
I'd like to go to bed now. It's not just the sun
- tion, and that makes it le - gal. Now, I find the ex - cu -

Am
Dm
F
— that is hurt - in' my head now. I'm not tryin' to say —
- ses o - ver - whelm - ing - ly fee - ble. You go to the doc -
A
Dm
F
— that I'm smell - in' of ro - ses, but when will we tire —
- tor, you need — pills for sleep - ing, well, if you can con - vince —
Am
Dm
F
— of put - tin' shit up our nos - es? I don't like stay - in' up, —
— him, then I guess that's not cheat - ing. So your daught - er's de - pressed? -

A
Dm
F
stay-in' up past the sun-light. It's meant to be fun
We'll get her straight on the Pro-zac. But lit-tle do you know
Am
Gm
B♭
F
C
and this just does-n't feel right.
she al-rea-dy takes crack.
Why can't we all, all just be hon-
Gm
B♭
Csus4
C
Gm
B♭
-est, and ad-mit to our-selves that ev-'ry-one's on it? From grown pol-i-ti-

F C Gm B♭ Csus4 C
-cians, to young ad - ol - es - cents, pres-crib-ing them-selves an - ti - de-press-
Gm B♭ F C Gm B♭
- ants. But how can we start to tack - le the prob - lem if you don't put your hands
Csus4 C Gm B♭ F C
up and ad - mit that you're on them? The kids are in dan - ger, they're all get - tin' hab-

Gm
B♭
Csus4
C
B♭
A5
3fr
- its, 'cause from what I can__ see,__ ev - 'ry - one's at it.
Dm
B♭
A5
Dm
Ev - 'ry - one's at it. Ev - 'ry - one's at
B♭
A5
Dm
To Coda
B♭
A5
N.C.
it. Ev-'ry - one's at it.
Dm
F
Am
Dm
F
Am

Dm F Am Dm F Am
Ev-'ry-one's at
Dm F A Dm F Am
it.
Dm F Am Dm F Am
D.S. al Coda
Gm B♭
Why can't we all,
Coda
B♭ A5
N.C.
it.

Not Fair

Words & Music by Lily Allen & Greg Kurstin

F
fif - teen times a day,__ he likes to make sure that I'm fine.__ You know I've
pret - ty_ damn hard done__ by, I spent ag - es giv - ing head.__ Then I re -
Dm
nev - er met a man__ who's made me feel quite so sec - ure,__ he's not like
- mem - ber all_ the nice__ things that you've ev - er said to me,__ may - be I'm
F
N.C.
all them oth - er boys__ they're all so dumb and im - mat - ure.__
just o - ver - re - act - ing, may - be you're the one__ for me.__
There's just one

Dm
thing that's get - ting in the way,___ when we go up to bed_
F
___ you're just no good, it's such a shame.________ I look in - to your
Dm
eyes, I want to get to know___ you, and then you make this
F
N.C.
noise and it's ap - par-ent it's___ all o - ver.

Gm
B♭
It's not fair and I think you're real - ly mean, I
F
C
think you're real - ly mean, I think you're real - ly mean. Oh,
Gm
B♭
you're sup posed to care, but you nev - er make me scream, you
C
nev - er make me scream. Oh,

Gm
B♭
it's not fair and it's real - ly not o - kay, it's
F
C
real - ly not o - kay, it's real - ly not o - kay. Oh,
Gm
B♭
you're sup - posed to care, but all you do is take, yeah,
C
To Coda
1.
all you do is take. 2. Oh, I

2.
C
Dm
F
Dm
F
There's just one

Dm
F
thing that's get - ting in the way, when we go up to bed you're just no
Dm
good, it's such a shame. I look in - to your eyes, I want to get to know
F
you, and then you make this noise and it's ap - par - ent it's all o -
D.S. al Coda
Coda
C
F
- ver.

The Fear

Words & Music by Lily Allen & Greg Kurstin

F/E♭
B♭/D
B♭m/D♭
and fuck loads of dia - monds, I heard peo - ple die while they're try - ing to find
- ter 'cause I'm pack ing plas - tic, and that's what makes my life so fuck-ing fan - tas -
F
F/E♭
B♭/D
them. And I'll take my clothes off and it will be shame - less, 'cause ev - 'ry - one knows
- tic. And I am a wea - pon of mas - sive con - sump - tion and it's not my fault
B♭m/D♭
F
F/E♭
it's how you get fam - ous. I'll look at the Sun and I'll look in the Mir -
it's how I'm pro - grammed to func - tion. I'll look at the Sun and I'll look in the Mir -

B♭/D
B♭m/D♭
N.C.
F
ror. I'm on the right track, yeah, I'm on - to a win - ner.
ror. I'm on the right track, yeah, I'm on - to a win - ner
And I don't know
Dm
Am
what's right and what's real an - y - more.
F
Dm
E♭
6fr
And I don't know how I'm meant to feel an - y - more.
F
Dm
When do you think it will all be - come

Am
F
— clear?
'Cause I'm — be - ing ta -
Dm
E♭
6fr
To Coda
- ken o - ver by the — fear. —
1.
F
F/E♭
B♭/D
B♭m/D♭

2.
F
F/E♭
B♭/D
B♭m/D♭
F
F/E♭
B♭/D
B♭m/D♭
F
F/E♭
For-get a-bout guns and for-get am-u-ni-
B♭/D
B♭m/D♭
F
-tion, 'cause I'm kill-ing them all on my own lit-tle mis-sion. Now, I'm not a saint,

F/E♭
B♭/D
B♭m/D♭
but I'm not a sin - ner, and ev - 'ry - thing's cool as long as I'm get - ting thin -
F
D.S. al Coda
Coda
- ner. And I don't know
F
Dm
Am
F
Dm
E♭
6fr

22

Words & Music by Lily Allen & Greg Kurstin

G7
Cm
F7
I see that look in her face, she's
'Cause all she wants is a boy-friend,
A♭7
E♭
B♭/F
Cm
got that look in her eye. She's think-ing how did I get
she gets one-night stands. She's think-ing how did I get
F7
A♭
G7
here, and won-der-ing why.
here, I'm do-ing all that I can.
Fm
Cm
B♭
It's sad, but it's true, how so-ci-e-ty says her life is al-read-y o-

A♭ Gm Fm7 E♭
- ver. There's noth - ing to do and there's noth - ing to
B♭ B♭7 Fm
say. Un - til the man of her dreams
Cm B♭ A♭ Gm7
comes a - long, picks her up and puts her o - ver his shoul - der,

Fm7
E♭
6fr
B♭
E♭/B♭
6fr
B♭7
it seems so un - like - ly in this day and age.
Cm
3fr
F7
A♭
4fr
E♭
6fr
Cm
3fr
F7
A♭
4fr
G
Fm7
It's sad, but it's true,

Cm7
3fr
B♭
A♭
4fr
Gm7
3fr
— how so-ci-e-ty says — her life is al-read-y o - ver. —
Fm7
E♭
6fr
B♭
3
There's noth-ing to do — and there's noth-ing to — say. —
B♭7
Fm
Cm
3fr
— Un-til the man of her dreams — comes a-long, — picks her up —
B♭
A♭
4fr
Gm7
3fr
Fm7
— and puts her o - ver his shoul - der, — it seems so un-like-

E♭ B♭ E♭/B♭ B♭7 Fm7
6fr
3
- ly in this day and age. (Ah,
Cm7 B♭ A♭ Gm7 Fm7
3fr 4fr
ah, ah, ah, ah. Ooh, ooh,
E♭ B♭ E♭/B♭ B♭7 Fm7
6fr
ooh, ooh, ooh, ooh, ooh, ooh, ooh.)
(Ah, ah.)

I Could Say

Words & Music by Lily Allen & Greg Kurstin

Gmaj7/B
Em7
— be___ here for you,___ but that___ would be___ a lie___
— ha - ted my friends.___ You made___ me feel___ so guil-
Gsus4
G
___ and quite___ a point - less thing___ to do.___
- ty when___ I was___ run - nin'___ round with them.
D
Gmaj7/B
I could say___ that I'll___ al - ways have feel - ings for
And ev - 'ry - thing___ was al - ways a - bout___ be - ing cool.___

Em7
you, but I've got a life a - head of me and I'm
And now I've come to re - al - ise there's noth - ing
Gsus4
A7
G(add2)
on - ly twen - ty - two.
cool a - bout you at all.
Since you've gone,
F♯m
A
D
I've lost that chip on my shoul - der.

G
F♯m
A
Since you've gone, I feel like I've got-ten old-
G(add2)
F♯m
- er. And now you've gone, it's as if the whole
A
D
G
wide world is my stage. And now you've gone,

F♯m
A
D/A
A7
To Coda ⊕
it's like I've been let out of my cage.
D
Am7
Ah,
C
ah,
ah.

Em
D
Am7
Ah,
ah,
C
Em
ah.

N.C.
D.S. al Coda
Ah.
Coda
D
Gmaj7/B
Em7
Gsus4
G
D

Never Gonna Happen

Words & Music by Lily Allen & Greg Kurstin

N.C.
Dm
And please can you stop call - ing, 'cause its's get - ting real - ly bor - ing and I've
Now I know you feel be - trayed, but it't been a week since I got laid. This does - n't
3
Gm
A7
told you I don't wan - na be friends.
mean that I don't think you're a fool.
Be - lieve me when I tell you that I
But I don't un - der - stand what else a
A
nev - er wan - na see you a - gain.
girl in my po - si - tion's to do.
D
A
How on earth could I be an - y more ob - vi - ous?

It never really did, and now it's never gonna happen with the
G
D
N.C.
D
two of us.
I don't under-stand
A/G
A
what it is that you're chasing after.
But it
makes me really sad to hear you sound so desp-'rate, it just

G
D/F♯
1.
N.C.
2, 3.
N.C.
makes it hard - er.
2. I can
D
A
Da da da da da da da da da da da da da da.
G
D
N.C.
Da da da da da da da da da da da da da da.
D
A/G
A
Da da da da da da da da da da da da da da.

Da da da da da da da da da da da
G
D/F♯
N.C.
Dm
da da da.
I know it's rath - er ug - ly, 'cause I
Gm
know that you still love me, and this is - n't an - y kind of ex - cuse; but
A
D.S. to fade
I don't love you, I don't love you.

Back To The Start

Words & Music by Lily Allen & Greg Kurstin

N.C.
You al - ways were, and you al - ways will be, the tall - er and pret - ti - er one.
B7/D#
Em
C
People seem to love you,
G
D
Em
they grav - i - tate to - wards you.
That's why I start - ed to hate
C
A
B
you so much, and I just com - plete - ly ig - nored you.

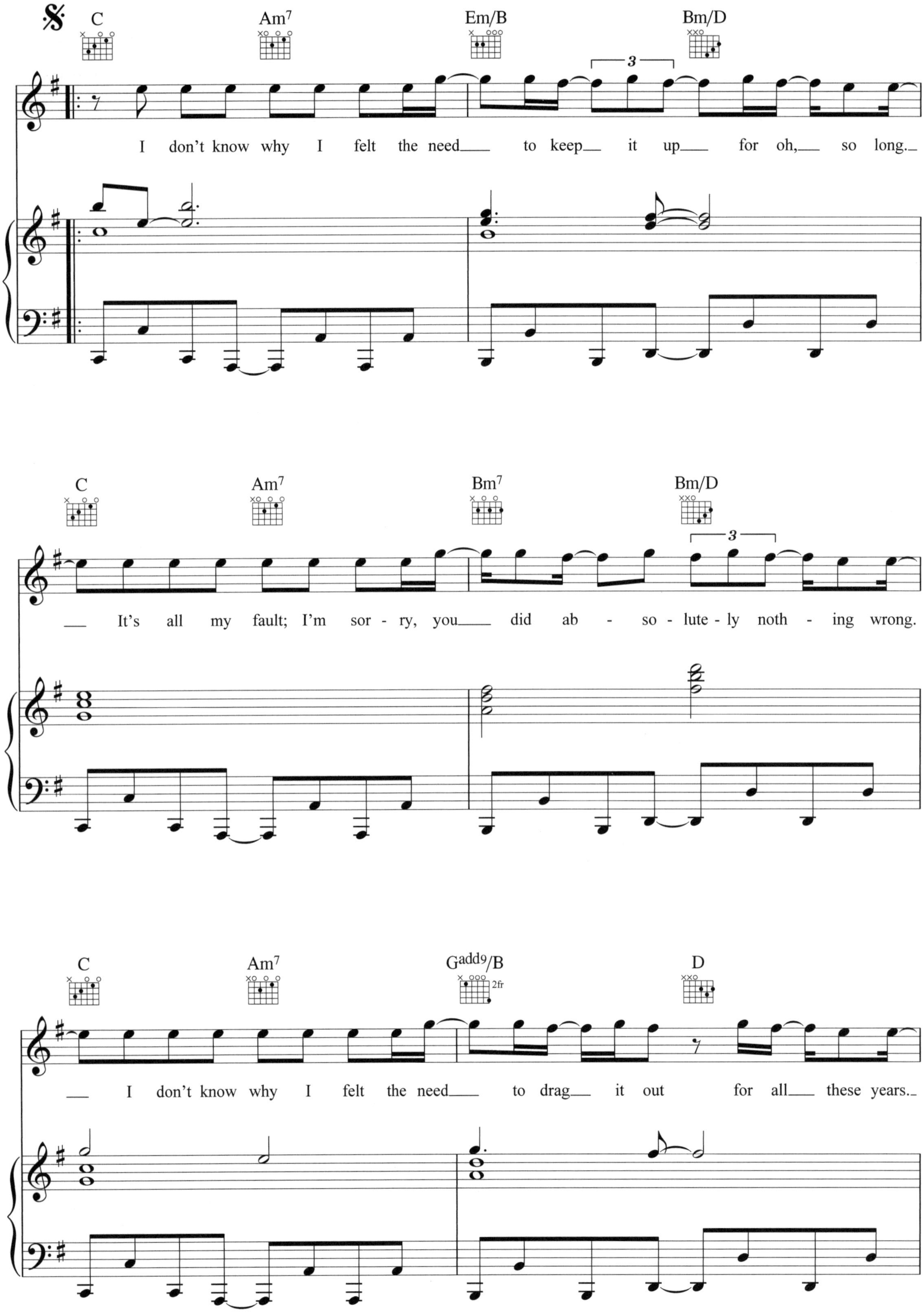
C
Am7
Em/B
Bm/D
3
I don't know why I felt the need___ to keep___ it up___ for oh,___ so long.___
C
Am7
Bm7
Bm/D
3
___ It's all my fault; I'm sor - ry, you___ did ab - so - lute - ly noth - ing wrong.
C
Am7
Gadd9/B
2fr
D
___ I don't know why I felt the need___ to drag___ it out for all___ these years.___

C Am C/B B7
— All the pain— I've caused— you, the con - stant flow of— the tears.
C Am7 Em/B Bm/D
Be - lieve me when I say— that I can - not a - pol - o - gise— e - nough,—
Am/C Am7 Bm7 Bm/D
— when all you ev - er want - ed from— me was a to - ken of— my love.
3
3

C
Am7
Gadd9/B
2fr
D
And if it's not too late, could you please find it deep with - in your heart
C
Am
C/B
B7
Em
to try and go back, and go back to the start.
Ah, ah,
C
G
D
ah, ah.
Go back to the start.

Em
C
G
To Coda
Ah, ah, ah, ah.
1.
B7/D#
Em
Am/C
2. I've been so e - vil, with my
G
D5
2fr
Em
con-stant in - va - sions.
But you made it so ea -

Am/C
G
B7/D♯
- sy for me, you al - ways rise to the oc - ca - sion.
Em
Am/C
G
I'll al-ways pull you up on ev - 'ry stu - pid thing that you say.
D5
2fr
Em
Am/C
But I found it so en - ter - tain - ing,

2.
A
B
B7/D#
mess-ing a-round with your head.
Go back to the start.
Em
C
G
Ah, ah, ah, ah.
D
Em
C
Go back to the start.
Ah, ah, ah,
G
B7/D#
N.C.
ah.

B7/D#
Em
Am/C
G
3. This is not just a song, I in - tend to put these words in - to ac -
D
Em
Am/C
- tion. I hope that it sums up the way that I feel

D.S. al Coda
Coda
A
B
B7/D#
to your sat - is - fac - tion.
Em
C
G
D
Em
C
G
B7/D#
(echo)

Fuck You

Words & Music by Lily Allen & Greg Kurstin

A A6 B6 B B6 B
of all the hat - red you har - bour.
well, that's not how you'll find it.
Eadd9 E Eadd9 E C#m(add9) C#m
4fr
2. So you say it's not o - kay to be gay, well, I think you're just ev -
4. Do you, do you real - ly en - joy liv - ing a life that's so hate -
5. You say you think we need to go to war; well, you're al - rea - dy in
C#m(add9) C#m F#m(add9) F#m F#m(maj7) F#m
- il. You're just some rac - ist who can't tie my la - ces,
- ful? 'Cause there's a hole where your soul should be, you're los - ing con trol of it,
one. 'Cause it's peo - ple like you that need to get slew,

A
A6
B6
B
B6
B
N.C.
your point of view is me - di - ev - al.
and it's real - ly dis - taste - ful.
no one wants your o - pi - nion.
E
G♯
4fr
Fuck you, fuck you ve - ry, ve - ry much.
C♯m
4fr
'Cause we hate what you do, and we hate your whole crew, so
B
E
please don't stay in touch.
Fuck you,

G♯
4fr
fuck you ve - ry, ve - ry much. 'Cause your words
C♯m
4fr
3
don't trans - late, and it's get - ting quite late, so please
B
To Coda
1.
2.
don't stay in touch.
G
B
(Fuck you, fuck you, fuck you. Fuck you, fuck

Em
you, fuck you.)
Fuck you.
Coda
D.S. al Coda
8va
E
G♯
4fr
Fuck you.
Fuck you.
C♯m
4fr
B
Repeat to fade
Fuck you.

Who'd Have Known

Words & Music by Lily Allen & Greg Kurstin

Fmaj7/A
E♭
E♭6
6fr
B♭
the stairs. And I pre-tend-ed I was sleep-ing, and I was hop-ing you would creep in with me.
F
2. You put your arm a-round my shoul-der, and it was if the room got
3. I have-n't left here for days now, and I'm be - com-ing a-mazed
4. Instrumental till *
cold - er; and we moved clos-er in to - geth - er, and start - ed talk - ing 'bout the
how you're quite af - fec-tion-ate in pub - lic; in fact, your friend said it made
Gm7
3fr

F
Fmaj7/A
weath - er. You said to - mor - row would be fun, and we could watch A Place
her feel sick. And e-ven though it's mov-ing for-ward, there's just the right a-mount of
E♭
6fr
B♭
In The Sun. I did-n't know where this was go - ing, when you kissed me.
awk-ward; and to-day you ac - ci - dent-'lly call me ba - by.
*
F
Am
Dm
F/C
Are you mine, are you mine? 'Cause I'd stay here all the time,
Gm7
3fr
B♭/F
E♭
6fr
Dm
Cm
3fr
E♭/B♭
6fr
watch - ing tel - ly, drink - ing wine.

F Am Dm F/C
Who'd have known? Who'd have known? When you flash up on my phone,
Gm7 3fr B♭/F
1.
C
I no long - er feel a - lone, no long - er feel a - lone.
E♭ 6fr Dm Cm 3fr E♭/B♭ 6fr F
2, 3.
C F Am
Let's just stay, let's just stay.

Dm F/C Gm7 B♭/F
I wan-na lie in bed all day, we'll be laugh-ing all the way.
E♭ Dm Cm E♭/B♭ F Am
You told your friends, they all know
Dm F/C Gm7 B♭/F
we ex-ist but we're tak-ing it slow. Now let's just see how we go,
C E♭ Dm Cm E♭/B♭ F
D.S. al Fine
Fine
let's see how we go.

Chinese

Words & Music by Lily Allen & Greg Kurstin

C
F
Fmaj7
I wait for an hour or so at the car - ou - sel.
I cry at the thought of be - ing a - lone, and then
Gm
Dm(add9)
I have a cig - a - rette to pass the time, 'cause the traf - fic's hell.
I won - der how long it - 'll take till I'm home a - gain.
B♭
Gm
C
B♭ (hold)
Ah.

F
Am
I don't want anything more than to see your face
Cm7
when you open the door. You'll make me beans on toast and a nice cup of tea
Gm7
3fr
C7sus4
3fr
C7
F
and we'll get a chinese and watch T. V. To-mor-row we'll take
Am
the dog for a walk, and in the afternoon then may-be we'll

Cm7
Gm7
3fr
talk. I'll be ex - haust - ed so I'll pro - bab - ly sleep and we'll get a chi - nese
To Coda
1.
C7sus4
3fr
C7
F
Fsus2
Fsus4
F7
and watch T. V.
2.
F
Fsus2
Fsus4
F5
F7
B♭/F
F

F
Fmaj7
Gm
3fr
I___ know___ it does-n't seem so___ fair,___
Dm
B♭
D.S. al Coda
but I'll send_ you a post - card when I get there.___
Coda
F
Fsus2
Fsus4
F5
F7
B♭/F
F
N.C.

Him

Words & Music by Lily Allen & Greg Kurstin

Am
A
When he looks down on us, I won - der what he sees.
Do you reck-on he's ev - er been done for tax e - va - sion?
F
F/E
F/D
F/A
B♭
2. Do you think he'd think the things we do are a waste of time?
4. Do you think he's an-y good at re-mem - ber-ing peo - ple's names?
5. Instrumental till Coda
F
F/E
F/D
F
B♭
May - be he'd think that we are get-ting on just fine.
Do you think he's ev-er tak - en smack or co - caine?
F
F/E
F/D
F
B♭
Do you think he's skint or fi - nan-cial-ly se - cure?
I don't im-ag - ine he's ev-er been su-i - ci - dal.

Am
A
And, come e - lec - tion time, I won - der who he'd vote for.
His fav - 'rite band is Cree - dence Clear - wat - er Re - vi - val.
Gm7
3fr
Dm
Gm7
3fr
Dm
Ev - er since he can re - mem - ber, peo - ple have died in his good
(Instrumental continues)
C
Gm
C
A
name. Long be - fore that Sep - tem - ber, long be - fore hi - jack - ing planes.
Gm7
3fr
Dm
Gm7
3fr
Dm
He's lost the will, he can't de - cide, he does - n't know who's right or wrong.

C Gm C A
To Coda
But there's one thing that he's sure of, this has been go-ing on too long.
1. F F/E F/D F/A B♭
Ah.
2. F F/E F/D F/A
Ah.
B♭ F F/E F/D F B♭
D.S. al Coda
Ah.
Coda
Gm7 3fr Dm Gm7 3fr Dm
Ev-er since he can re-mem-ber, peo-ple have died in his good

C Gm C A
name. Long be - fore___ that___ Sep - tem - ber, long be - fore___ hi - jack - ing planes.___
Gm7 Dm Gm7 Dm
3fr
___ He's lost the will,___ he can't de - cide,___ he does - n't know___ who's right___ or wrong.___
C Gm C A
___ But there's one___ thing that___ he's sure___ of, this has been go - ing on___ too long.___
F F/E F/D F/A B♭ F

He Wasn't There

Words & Music by Lily Allen & Greg Kurstin

C6
G
It did-n't mat-ter if he let me down,
-wife. I know you would-n't but there is no need,
strong. And just in case you ev-er thought I would,
F
C6
I did-n't care a-bout the lies. All I knew was that he
no need to a-pol-o-gize. Be-cause I know you al-ways
I would-n't change you for the world. Be-cause I know you al-ways
G
F
C6
loved me ve-ry much, he was my he-ro in dis-guise.
loved me ve-ry much; you are my he-ro in dis-guise.
loved me ve-ry much, I'll al-ways be your lit-tle girl.
B♭
F
C
I'm so pleased I nev-er gave up on him. Oh well, you

B♭
F
C
would-n't be-lieve some of the things that he did.
B♭
F
C
And ev-'ry-one said "You have to give him some time."
D7
F
G
C
And I'm glad that I gave it to him, 'cause now ev-'ry-thing's fine.
1.
N.C.
2. Now you see I nev-er
2.
N.C.
3. You might have thought you did-n't
3.
N.C.

1 2 3 4 5 6 7 8 9